To: Badger Family♪
Edge of the Blue Lake
Under the Forest

From Chirri and Chirra

One cloudy day, Chirri and Chirra
decide to go out on their bicycles.

Kaya Doi

# Chirri & Chirra
## The Rainy Day

Translated from the Japanese by
**David Boyd**

*Enchanted Lion Books*
NEW YORK

*Dring-dring, dring-dring!*
It's already starting to rain.

Café
Umbrella

OPEN .... RAINY DAYS

CLOSED .... SUNNY DAYS

Pedaling along, they discover a shop. What luck!
The sign says it's only open on rainy days.

Sit anywhere
you please.

Inside, the walls are covered with paintings.
The frames all have different shapes and
colors, each with a picture of rain inside.

Oh, wait...
They're windows!

Their drinks come with bowls of frozen raindrop candy.

Chirri orders the chrysanthemum tea with lemon marmalade and Chirra orders the peppermint tea with green-apple syrup.

This must be a shop for watching
the rain while drinking tea.

They even sell
rainy-day items of
all shapes and colors.

Chirri and Chirra find
the raincoats that they like best.

When they leave the shop,
the rain is falling even
harder than before.

*Dring-dring, dring-dring!*
They pedal faster and faster. Meanwhile,
the rain falls harder and harder.

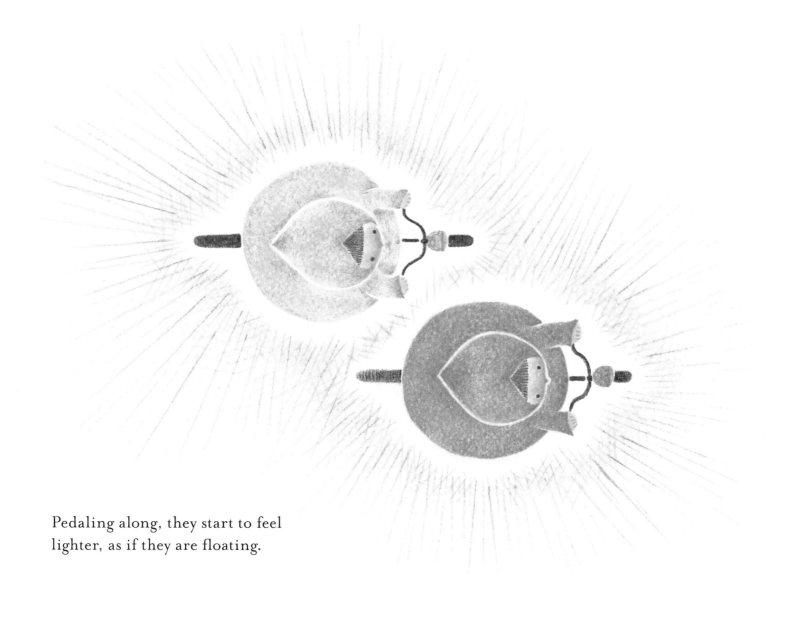

Pedaling along, they start to feel
lighter, as if they are floating.

When they look up at the sky, they don't see any rain.
Has it really stopped?

Oh, wait...
The rain hasn't stopped.
It's falling from below!

*Dring-dring, dring-dring!*
They ride their bicycles
over the upside-down rain.

What luck!
A shop with a window
on the second story.

When they go inside,
they see stamps in all
colors and shapes.

Chirri and Chirra
buy the stamps that
they like best.

This way, please.

Down the stairs...

They discover a happy scene in the upside-down rain.

*Dring-dring, dring-dring!*
They start pedaling again.

What is everybody doing over there?
Have they found something special?

Look! Gummy gumdrops dangling
from the branches, ripe and sparkling.

Chirri and Chirra take one piece each
and pop them in their mouths.
*Chomp chomp, nom nom, yum yum.*

Just then, the sky gets brighter.
The sun is breaking through the clouds.

The upside-down rain has ended.
But how will they ever get down?

Just then, Chirra and Chirra start feeling lighter,
as if they're floating. The gummy gumdrops
are growing as big as balloons!

The others float with them, too.
Gently, gently.

*Dring-dring, dring-dring!*
What a wonderful day in the rain.

The End

Born in Tokyo, Kaya Doi graduated with a degree in design from Tokyo Zokei University.
She got her start in picture books by attending the Atosaki Juku Workshop, a program at a Tokyo bookshop.
Prolific and popular, Doi has created many wonderful books. She now lives in Chiba Prefecture
and maintains a strong interest in environmental and animal welfare issues.

David Boyd is Assistant Professor of Japanese at the University of North Carolina at Charlotte.
His translations have appeared in *Monkey Business International*, *Granta*, and *Words Without Borders*,
among other publications.

*Enchanted Lion Books*
NEW YORK

www.enchantedlion.com

First edition, published in 2021 by Enchanted Lion Books,
248 Creamer Street, Studio 4, Brooklyn, New York 11231
Text and illustrations copyright © 2019 by Kaya Doi
English translation rights arranged with Alicekan Ltd. through Japan UNI Agency, Inc.
All rights reserved under International and Pan-American Copyright Conventions.
A CIP record is on file with the Library of Congress. ISBN 978-1-59270-307-4
Printed in China by RR Donnelley Asia Printing Solutions Ltd.
1 3 5 7 9 10 8 6 4 2